AF582495

Sexolitude

Efraín José Martínez Meneses

Published in March, 2016
2 st edition
Cataca Productions
Yellow House Publishing Group
Printed in Colombia
ISBN:978-958-59392-4-0

DEDICATION

To my daughter, who is everything to me. I hope she reads this book after turning 18 and discovers that every step I take is her step. There are landscapes I want to tell her about and feelings I want to describe to her.

"What can a poet do without pain? He needs it as much as the typewriter." Charles Bukowski.

This book is made of real people's stories. Do you have a story that could be in Sexolitude II? If you do, you will receive a free copy of the book once it's produced. Reality is always better than fiction, and literature is a mirror in which we reflect to know what to heal. When we read ourselves, we are able to understand and forgive more easily.

First beginning.

"You suffer from sexolitude," I said. More to make myself seem interesting than because I actually believed it. Combining two words that affect 99.9% of humanity, using those two simple generalities to appear mystical, pure cheap fortune-teller psychology. With the evident intention of getting into bed with Camila, trusting that a bit of the apparent nonsense of sapiosexuality might make some sense.

She looked it up on her phone and couldn't find the meaning in the Oxford English Dictionary, only on an obscure blog where the word was defined as something related to masturbation.

"If it's not in the OED, it doesn't exist and therefore I can give it whatever definition I want and popularize it to the point that it's recognized someday. Besides, my definition of the perverse and indissoluble alliance between sex and loneliness is more beautiful and complex, one that doesn't depend solely on whether you share your solitude or your lust, whether you contract them like a "Venereal disease, or if you're just messed up inside," I said.

I kept trying to devise my strategy to get her into bed, entangling her in a sudden and lurid explanation.

"Do you remember I told you about Nineth's dad? A tall black man with a prominent belly that made the second and third buttons of his shirt struggle. He was the town's photographer. I never knew his name; even when greeting him, I called him Nineth's dad. Foto Medina, his business, was right across from the funeral home of 'Deadface.' He was another great character, a caricature, a cliché of the macabre made flesh: sunken eyes, raccoon-like dark circles, 190 cm tall, straight slicked-back hair, pale, thin as a wardrobe, and an Adam's apple that made him look like a turkey.

Well, when I went to Foto Medina, I would rush past the funeral home's door. I still remember Deadface's bad habit of placing the coffins at such an angle that everyone inside, and those of us who accidentally glanced in, could see the face of the deceased through the small window of the coffin. The closed eyes of the dead that I saw still gaze at me.

I would arrive at the Medinas', and while Nineth fetched her notebook, I would absently look over the black-and-white photos. She always found me with teary eyes, the light tear mixing with the inevitable sweat. She never said anything. Perhaps I wasn't the only one saddened by the photograph taken by her grandfather on the day of the banana massacre. In that photo: a mother shields her dead son's body from the absurd kicks and blows of the soldiers' rifle butts, soldiers sent by President Abadía to dissolve the workers' protests, pleasing the U.S. government, and making a clear point that the coastal soldiers often ended up, as usual, in revelry and carousing with their fellow countrymen, who were workers of the United Fruit Company. In the background of the photo, on some steps leading to the town square, you can see a gringo dressed in an impeccable white suit and white hat. He's covering his mouth and nose with a white handkerchief. Perhaps the smell of dried blood and the cloud of flies feasting on death bothered him. My grandmother used to say that the devil must be a gringo and his demons, cachacos, you can bet on it."

"Did Gabo tell that story?" "So, did that really happen?"

"Of course, it happened, and it keeps happening, only now there's no one left to write about it. Gabo and Cepeda Samudio are gone."

"You know, the photos the Medinas took conveyed something; you could feel the heat and boredom of the plaster saints in the Holy Week processions just by looking at the black-and-white images. The fire of the fireworks seemed to spark and spread the joy of the 'crazy cows' celebrations in the fair days' pictures. You could see the tension in the faces of the photographed families, knowing that having a photo taken "...was a major event, a time to prepare, knowing that photos were forever, a way to conquer death and oblivion."

"I never had the money to buy a camera back then. Today, I'm not interested anymore. How many passions has poverty killed in this world? But I realize that, in essence, I'm trying to do the same thing. Capture moments in text."

"I'm a 'textographer,'" I applauded my own cleverness. "While they discover a machine to store and transmit the sensations of a moment, I do it with words. People sometimes aren't able to write themselves."

"Describe themselves, you mean."

"Cami, I said it right: write themselves; describing is another thing: a narrative act that outlines a recipe; a concoction of things listed to remember, not to reminisce or address the 'self,' which is beyond flesh and time. As Mctaggart rightly says, though you might not like that kind of literature, the image is not in the object but in the observer; that's where it forms."

"And even if you don't believe me, with my writings, I've seen them cry on this balcony, from where I've seen the neighbor's wife masturbate when she 'accidentally' leaves the curtains open (I can't hear or say the word balcony without recalling that scene). When they read what I wrote about them, they see themselves, they identify."

"That's what I wanted to say," they tell me. "That's me," they recognize.

"I do text therapy, Camila, admit it, Camila."

"Every person should have an album of textographies, just like they have a photo album. And don't come at me with that nonsense that it's a diary, because it's not."

"Does everyone in your town talk so much shit? Professor José also tells me all sorts of stories to explain any nonsense," Camila replied.

Camila is a beautiful woman, slender body, and a smile like Julia Roberts, but local. When she has a boyfriend, she's more faithful than Eve, but a day after a breakup, she turns into a cynical nymphomaniac: she sleeps with the doorman of her building, professors, bartenders at social song taverns, taxi drivers, gropers in crowds, perverts from sex classifieds on the Internet, friends' dads and brothers, police officers, basically anyone with a penis.

She broke up with her boyfriend Raúl yesterday. He's a good guy, but she's not sure she wants to get married, and Raúl proposed. Honestly, it's not that I feel empathy for Raúl; I just want to be the release for Camila's temporary and almost contractual fidelity, but she doesn't sleep with friends. Damn it! Codes of honor and prejudices in a nymphomaniac, just what I needed. We talked for a long time, watched Italian porn, and ate salty cookies with caramel. She's already feeling the emptiness of sex, well, more than sex, the addiction to it. She doesn't want to go back to trying to distract her existential problems and her heart with penises.

It could be worse. Some people acquire really harmful addictions like alcohol, drugs, literature, or fat. She confesses to me that sex distracts her, "It's like going to the movies; it isolates you for a moment and you're happy, but then when you leave, when you cross the theater door and the light becomes strong, the real world pours in like a cascade of shit. Well, that's what it's like when you have an orgasm. The world and its details become visible, and once again you're alone with a bundle of flesh with a name and a family, getting in the way in bed. Anyway, even though I feel this way now, I know that tomorrow I'll ride someone else. That's how addictions are."

"You're right." "About what?"

"I suffer from sexolitude."

"You're good at this crap, but I'm still not going to blow you."

She smoked a small joint she had just bought from a guy nicknamed "Zamba," like the Argentinean dance, not the Brazilian Samba (he always makes that clear). He sells all kinds of weed, and I've never seen him sober. She thought his semen must taste like weed, but she found out it didn't. The truth is I drink Coca-Cola all day, but she won't taste mine. She finished smoking, put in eye drops to clear her eyes, chewed cardamom seeds for her breath, and drank a lot of water.

"Let them call me a whore, but not a pothead. Jesus never talked about potheads, but he did talk about whores," she said as she closed the door behind her.

Everyone tells me I'm good at understanding people, which is really absurd because all I do is listen and laugh. Maybe it's because sometimes what defines you isn't what you're good at, but what you're bad at, and what I'm really bad at is judging. Even if I hear about perversions, painful and fatal mistakes, I'm not shocked or fazed; I try to protect them from their own guilt, their own demons, and unhappiness. My friends refer their friends to me, and I've gained a certain reputation among a circle of hipsters, hippies, punks, and the occasional frustrated executive, which hasn't made me any money, but my sexolitude (if such a thing exists) is soothed by listening to their stories. It's my addiction: their crazy tales, their broken souls, their disordered lives, their agony, the unique and original ways they get lost. One day their spirit hurts, the next day their genitals, and sometimes both.

I like to tell others about the ruins carried by the people who come to me, and among them, I also tell them to make them feel better, to let them know they're not alone. That there are others just as or more messed up than they are, and that the mask of perfection we wear daily is a heavy burden for such a fragile life.

I never reveal their real names when I recount their struggles or adventures, to protect the identity of the reader, because I'm sure my patients would like everything to be known all at once. They would feel even freer and become pioneers in that new world where the pursuit of perfection is a destructive fiction. The real disease is not allowing oneself to fail, not allowing oneself to be human, and not allowing that combination of god and animal to coexist within, without one killing the other.

My therapy against that ocean of loneliness and desire is writing what my "patients" tell me. I don't diagnose, but they start to heal, healing me in the process. I lend them my voice, and when they read their own stories, they begin to find peace—not direction, as they'll never find that. Maybe it's that human vice of having answers for others and not for oneself. By observing the tales, the sweet prose, the furious prose, they can, from the outside, see the map of their lives and know they will reach the end of their journey, whatever the route may be. And the best part? Enjoying it.

Every story they tell me, every story we discuss, is real and charged with the sincerity of people who have nothing to gain by lying, of people who are capable of being genuinely authentic amid tribulations or peace, stripped of divine idealism.

I'm not a writer (maybe I'm a textographer), I'm not a psychologist, I'm not coherent. But in a world where a video of a turtle opening a sliding door has 800 million views on YouTube, any disproportionate and senseless act can lead us to propagate the most implausible idea and create images that ride on words.

Hopefully, these stories from those I insolently call "patients" will help you appreciate your own diverted paths and find yourself among the billions who get lost daily in their own condition, which turns out to be a world for all.

TEXTOGRAPHIC ALBUM

PATIENT 001:

Juanita is 28 years old and lives in Manrique. She is a corporate executive at a cell phone company. Her life was full of hardships. Juanita is beautiful and has achieved a comfortable economic position. Now she thinks she deserves something better in her life. Perhaps she means her husband, although she avoids the subject when I ask.

Textographies of Juanita

01

(Treat Me Gently by Soda Stereo, interpreted by someone who didn't understand it). Juanita has a lover; her husband is boring and monotonous. But Juanita's lover is another woman's boring and monotonous husband. She knows that it's the possession of people that turns them into furniture. When the priest or pastor or notary or some motherfucker in Las Vegas says, "I now pronounce you husband and wife," a metamorphosis happens as if by magic: both become mechanisms of a machine, and the machine calculates that they will always be there until they wear out; the gear knows that after one tooth comes another, and another, and another, infinitely. Juanita knows this too and acknowledges that she will not be the one to break the social order of things, the script of normality that is written in stone. Moreover, she has never been outwardly rebellious, only the kind of rebel who remains silent and suffers from heartburn, insomnia, and liver damage, but never raises her fist or her voice.

The truth is she has a lover, and he won't be the last. She suffers from loneliness, that constant feeling of having something unfinished with someone or something, but without knowing what that something is, and worse, without knowing who that someone is.

She looks into her lovers' eyes and knows that behind them lies loneliness, that there is no surprise, that the passion will last until one of them looks beyond and confirms the prediction.

After sex, covered in semen even in her ears, and with that acidic taste in her mouth that is exquisite during but tastes like shit after the orgasm, she smokes a cigarette while it dries on her face, turning into crusts on her skin and soul. Her lovers, after a brief recovery nap, see her with her lost gaze, naked, exhaling smoke slowly. They caress her body just to caress it because after ejaculation, all that's left is skin, muscles, and guts: the goddess vanishes like a ninja. They play at removing the crusts of semen from her face, feeling like alpha males marking their territory, while she feels only that she is a territory of untamed beasts that devour men, but that someone has wisely set just limits for her so that every now and then, the beasts believe there is a horizon beyond the skin, beyond the gaze.

And who removes the crusts from her heart? She gets up and dresses before her lover does, quickly fleeing the place; guilt also comes after the orgasm. She kisses him quickly, without tongue, and prays, as she exits the motel door, that something will keep her from falling into temptation again. But she arrives home, and her husband complains about the time she got home, complains about the food, complains about the bills, complains about her lackluster sex, complains about her family, complains because she doesn't complain. He is a normal being, one of those born in September, who has his life planned out, who counts even his bowel movements and believes in psychologists. She, on the other hand, is the rock with eyes, who one day discovers she is a rock and cannot bear her immobility; she doesn't find herself, doesn't understand herself, she only knows what doesn't make her happy, and it's almost everything. She goes to bed without eating, wishing he would notice her smell of sex, leaving her phone in plain sight so he makes the mistake of looking at it. She is fed up with her life, and he makes it worse; he wouldn't understand her disarray, her melancholy. He uses suppositories suggested by the pastor of his church to cleanse his soul; he is such a normal being that even his god must have forgotten him. He is the result of the mass production of humans, a straight-line segment, the digitalization of boredom, of the mundane.

She chases glory, even though she likes the song that says, "I never pursued glory…" when Serrat and Sabina sing it. He lies down beside her with his endless diatribe, and she tries to sleep, but the hatred for that mosquito buzzing in her ear only allows her to pretend she's already asleep to see if he stops bothering her.

The next day, they both get up as if nothing happened, give each other a goodbye kiss as they leave for work, and everything starts over. Juanita has a lover...

Patient 002:

Ricardo lives with his mother, is about to turn 40, and drives one of the Bello-Medellín routes. He's looking for a wife, but his finances don't allow it, and his mother needs care due to her advanced age. He has embraced rebellion (he admits this himself) as a defense mechanism against what he calls "a shitty life." He blames his poetry for driving women away, but he can't help gifting poems as soon as he meets them.

Textographies of Ricardo

01

I am not an exceptional man; I fit perfectly into the "all men are the same" category of women with broken dreams. In fact, I quickly tire of their inhuman desires mixed with rabid resignation. I walk the streets like a trained animal, discreetly looking at butts and chewing on some recycled poem or prose; Neruda, Benedetti, Cortázar... The same stuff pretty girls consume on social media, as far as their hair extensions allow them to feel above average. I don't meet anyone's expectations; whoever judges me is the one who loses. Here, there is only fury fed by orgasms with tears and other chimerical details. I burn suggestion manuals and explode like fireworks in the definitions of what I should be. At first glance and repeatedly, I am what loneliness aspires to be when it grows up: almost pure air, the wheel that didn't turn, one of the many truths pissed on by stray dogs, and ultimately, the feeling of being lost but not wanting to be found.

02

... Childhood should be a place, not a time... To take you to mine, to immerse myself in yours, to return, to keep it a secret, to wait for me there and wait for you... And not to pretend... Nor to pretend. Let's go on vacation there, where Dad is young and Mom smiles... Without damn Barjavel and his temporal paradoxes... Let me know if you manage to go... I'll bring the salt and pepper for the guavas...

03

Nostalgia shakes off the water like a bird on these

rainy days... Mmm... let's correct that... like a dog... Mmm, well, it just shakes... Just nostalgia, and that's it... Actually, these words are crossed out... You don't read them... I haven't written them... I didn't think them... They ceased to be... They are not... They never were... Ah! someone take them away from me... I can't stand their fluttering like tiny insects.

Patient 003:

Juan B. Son of a stern, alcoholic policeman, is a teacher at a school in Copacabana that often delays payments. He has large ears and thick lips. Only last year did he understand why his students would shout, "Big blimps, big blimps! Big blimps, big blimps!" when he approached the classroom. Juan thought it was because he is known for the number of exercises she assigns."

but what they were actually shouting was: "The big lips! The big lips!" He always tells the story of a model who looked at him at the Aguacatala metro station, a dull and meager story. He tells it, and standing in front of the waterfall of tears, he stops, smiles – more out of resignation than joy – and expresses that it's incredible that meeting a model who later died in surgery is the most exciting thing that ever happened to him. He believes the model liked him and regrets not having had the courage to ask for her phone number, something that happens to him often with many women. He wants a girlfriend; he's a good guy, a prince in a toad's body.

Textographies of Juan B.

01

At this age and with so many untamed demons, my father by this time had already mounted, bridled, and even castrated them. I hide mine during the day, like someone sweeping garbage under the rug; I work, talk to you, tell you I'm thinking of you, call my mom, rush home among the thousands of hurried workers doing the same, open the door, turn on the TV, and let them loose. I lock the door, don't answer calls, don't answer messages; pains, sorrows, lusts, euphoria, those are my demons' names. Dad would have dominated them, though I remember he also closed his door and latched it, to sleep "like a rock," he used to say.

Even back then, I had an inkling about congenital curses and the heap of absurd inheritances.

02

And how will we love each other if we don't know each other and don't even want to? She must be thinking of me, and she doesn't know my name nor do

I know hers. I see her from behind in my mind, with her hair down, looking out the window at a tree-lined street where children play who are neither hers nor mine, thinking that a man she knows nothing about is looking at her back… And sometimes she wants me to take her by the waist and whisper my name, and many times I do too, but we both remember how much we hate that domestic form of love, that subjugated love: that irrational yet accepted belonging, of ceasing to be oneself. So, she writes the same phrase on the fogged glass with her breath: love is the waiting. And she goes off to seek her princes without sphincters, her plush horses, and her lonely worlds. I leave the door ajar and wait for the princess who burned her ships and now wants us to watch the fire together from afar.

(And answering the question, we will love each other at times, only when we are lovers and stop being man and woman, just at times. Love is scarce, it's better to ration it).

03

(Butterfly Effect): An ugly man at the Aguacatala station encounters a stunning, unbelievable woman. He barely looks at her, sits down, and waits for the train. His dignity has taught him not to waste time tempting himself with delicacies he will never taste. She walks away insecure, checking her reflection, something is wrong. How could a guy with such a face and body not even notice her? That night, he sleeps like a rock, exhausted; being a math teacher isn't easy. She thinks about the ugly guy, hates him with all her heart, tossing and turning in bed, detesting every horrible feature: his broad face, pig-like cheeks, his laborer's back. The sun surprises her still tearing apart what has been shattered since birth. She gets up, looks in the mirror, and the sleepless night has given her bags and dark circles around her beautiful green eyes, along with a tiny trace of acne on her forehead. She picks up the phone, calls her surgeon friend who, having slept with her several times, is paying his small karma with free and unscheduled surgeries. She urgently wants a blepharoplasty for the bags and dark circles and, if possible, a light peeling for her acne.

At one in the afternoon, the ugly man turns on the TV; the news is going crazy over the death of a model in the operating room. Seeing the photo, he remembers she is the same woman from the station, "Even the damn worms eat better than I do," he mutters coldly under his breath.

04

I could swear she looked at me... and I thought about what people see when they look at each other, well, when they look at each other like she and I did, a gaze without a penis or a vagina, of dreams beyond quantities and magnitudes, of Oedipuses and Electras with oversized heads, the gaze of the dying who project the movie of their lives in fractions of seconds, in countless flashes... I could swear she looked at me and I loved her forever in that instant. I built magnificent universes, like when God created us in a blink, in a snotty sneeze, as exaggerated and obsolete as the love I was taught, like the love made with eyes, like the love that never discovers it's love and walks around with its butt in the air like an innocent and rowdy angel. I'll leave you now, I'm going to write something else about how tears are the blood of the soul... besides, I'm already in the phase that comes after the emotional orgasm and I'm thinking that maybe... You looked at me like one looks at strange creatures, nothing more, nothing more...

How do you now represent emptiness without the word? One pours into the other... Silence without the word? One calls to the other... Anyway, it's late and tomorrow we have to work.

05

I could have taken the known path and been common, writhing in the guts of society like a thin, harmless parasite, a man who knows where he's going; that's what women who know where they want to go ask for. I live in vertigo, in shifting realities, in forests where Little Red Riding Hood wouldn't dare get lost, scared but with a feigned smile that is already a wrinkle, already a tic, thinking every moment how late it has become to go back, to wear the beige pants and black loafers that the doctors in my town wore. Those men even knew the day they would die, never stumbling, not even walking backwards. Women loved them more than boiled plantain with cheese and let themselves be made love to in a fleeting missionary position, excited, ejaculating at the thought that their children would be born with a diploma rolled up in the umbilical cord. I perform a perverse, furious, animalistic, basic act, spending my feelings like a matchstick on sandpaper. It's not making love, rather it's a way of unmaking it, of melting it in friction, of punishing it, a sentimental and ostentatious wrestling match, sweaty, viscous, profane (I like that word, and confident men don't). How lost, how distant, how insecure, how immature, how bewildered and how volatile is the fate of those of us who had the brilliant idea not to choose a path. I finished the paragraph just to finish it. Everything is abrupt in anxiety. I have so much to tell you, but for today it's enough to blur myself before your eyes. The letters are raindrops falling on a fresh mural, swirling and carrying the diluted art down the drain, to mingle with the hatreds and wastes of big, hard cities like this one.

Patient 004:

Juan M. is a baker. He was on the rise, having set up two bakeries, but in 2010, chains and chains of bakeries with cheap products suddenly appeared, flooding the neighborhoods with their organized and well-located establishments. Although there were suspicions of these being front companies for money laundering, they remain, and they bankrupted Juan M. Since the bankruptcy, his wife treats him poorly, blames him for everything, adding to the collection of his own sorrows and missteps, the deterioration of their marriage.

Textography of Juan M.

01

"Absurd, that mating ritual where the male's partner rips off his head."

"Are you referring to the mantis?"

"No, what the mantis does isn't absurd because she does it immediately; it's benevolent, almost expiatory and purifying."

"You know what I mean, and I won't say it in front of so many people."

"If you knew me a little, that melancholic metaphor would seem simple to you."

Patient 005

Esmeralda studies at the National University. She hasn't told her mom about her recent lesbianism; she likes delicate, older women, especially those who are married. She wants to run away from home, but although she pretends to love freedom, she knows she can't discard the comforts her home provides. This resistance to herself keeps her in a constant state of conflict. She told me she is in love with a straight woman and gets excited touching her buttocks, pretending it's a normal hetero game between friends. She will never tell her, fearing she will lose her.

Textographies of Esmeralda

01

Out there, the world is falling apart, have you seen it? Sometimes I think light eyes can't see that.

Do I tend to your flowers while everything burns? Or make you a coffee?

Someday they will come for us, those who know we are happy. When they swallow everyone's dreams, they will come for us, pretty girl, and neither I nor the beings that protect us will be able to prevent it. These freshly made worlds are detectable, this scent of our sex spreads, it's a trail of good things, it's tear gas in the eyes of the resentful. They will come soon, and my only weapon will be a "fuck you" as I devour you with the last of my desire.

02

Soon those undefined things will come to lie beside you, to breathe your air, to drool on your pillow.

Though at first they will be terrifying, you will get used to them as you do to ridiculous fetishes, fake solitudes, and the stunted moans of neighboring lovers, you will get used to them.

You know, sleeping with demons, without spells, without panties, without love, saying that everything is normal, natural, almost human.

You understood so young that lust and heartbreak dress and undress the same, and soon, very soon, you will be that undefined thing that lies beside someone, breathes their air, and drools on their pillow...

Patient 006

Martín claims to be an ELN guerrilla. He studies at the University of Antioquia and you don't need to conduct any investigation for him to tell you, left and right, not without first warning you to keep it a secret, that he belongs to an urban cell of that armed group. After a speech about love and defending women's rights, I heard him say he doesn't like sex. I don't inquire about traumatic experiences in that regard; that would be too easy.

Textographies of Martín

01

After the mechanical genitality, to which I don’t attribute more significance than a sweaty handshake, only the moments that acquire value if they are unpredictable, profane, and unusual remain. That’s why I hate motels; because there’s no way to fool the mind, like the cow in its row of livestock sees a tunnel and loses hope of heading to a pasture and forage tasting party. Motels are cliffs of passions, crude trampolines for acrobats of the bump and grind, of the trinis, of the choclog choclog, of the wiki wiki, of the take that, circuses of sex, pantheons of surprise and mischief, there one only goes to perform. If it’s not corrupted, if it’s not perverted, sex is just a good aerobic exercise, but it doesn’t liberate or move.

02

"Love must not be allowed to die," asserts one of those academic experts on television. She shares the set with an angelologist (yes, an expert on angels, I know, WTF!!), and continues talking about the importance of details, saying it’s necessary to keep them up in a relationship, even after years of marriage, blah blah blah, until she gets to the only point of interest to the studio audience, which raises a murmur of giggles and throat-clearings, and of course, to us viewers: sex. She recites by heart the list of toys and acrobatics everyone already knows, but she has learned to say it eloquently, as if it were her discovery, implicitly acknowledging that passion is no longer within the bodies, but in objects, toys, outfits, that you have to search for it like one looks for oil, with drilling equipment, suction devices, and all kinds of chemicals. It crosses my mind that oblivion is more dignified than these antics, that the euthanasia of love is a good way to manage the population of mirages and anxieties. She emphasizes the costumes and recounts as an anecdote that her husband (happy or unhappy?) likes to see her dressed as a nurse. I'm sure she mentions it so we can all imagine her slender surgical body wrapped in a tiny outfit that's related to health only by a small red cross printed on it. Being desired by millions probably excites her a little; she puts on a falsely embarrassed face and smiles with feigned shame as they show her photos. She, with feigned surprise, asks them to explain how they got them. I turn off the TV; I already checked MTV and there's only a reality show about pathetic people who would sew a third testicle just to be on TV. On the History Channel, the last bastion of the somewhat comprehensible, they are trying to calculate the price of a piece of fossilized dinosaur crap. I lie on the couch, having triumphed over that river of shit. The divorced woman from the third floor yells at her son; we all know she is divorced because she rudely connects any trivial event in a conversation to her divorce, to further highlight her already evident availability, especially if the interlocutor is a heterosexual man with a lot, medium, little, or no sperm production. Bisexuals and even homosexuals with slips also have a chance. She was yelling at her son that she wouldn't buy him more toys, that he had a chest full of them and didn't use any; you must value what you have, she stressed, saying this after abandoning her husband for being a man without aspirations, a man without goals, a man without a defined life at 40. The boy was not yet in a position to understand the incoherence and low moral weight of his mother's authoritarian advice. I continued my little Sunday reflection on the sofa thinking that this is simply how we are from childhood; we play with that new object and soon abandon it, guilt and other bonds prevent us from throwing it away, but from childhood, we know it's no longer the same, that we cling to sugary fictions and that's why I firmly believe that in a perfect and lasting relationship, someone lies, someone hides, someone suffers, someone endures, someone is temporarily a fool, but averaging out a fool and a normal person is enough to make it viable, to round off near perfection. Maybe that undeniable, inescapable, natural reproductive programming turns us into something that waits to be recognized, to be made official; that we are just a sophisticated sex toy with the advanced option of poetizing about functions, secretions, and mixtures of viscous fluids. But well, you can stuff yourself with a mental suppository the size of Jupiter and believe that poets, those lonely chronic masturbators, are right when they irresponsibly talk about eternities and their amorous sophisms in these dimensions, because I won't deny it, in other dimensions it is totally possible, as Vinicius understood when he says: "Love is eternal while it lasts."

Patient 007

Professor José is from the Atlantic coast and lives in downtown Medellín. He fled with his family during the paramilitary violence and guerrilla threats in the 90s. Thanks to the education he received at the Terciarias Capuchinas nuns' school, he lives in a windowless apartment, the heat is unbearable, but for 200,000 pesos a month, it's impossible to find anything better. He's a professor, which sounds important, but the truth is he survives with a few hours here and there at different universities, institutes, and any garage that accepts his nonsense, as he himself says. "I've made such bad decisions in my life that I'm actually glad when things don't go as I want, it frees me from being guilty again of my ill-fated destiny," he now has that aphorism summarizing his life. He thinks a lot about absolutely everything, sleeps poorly, has lost many passions, and at 30 years old feels too old to dance reggaeton and says he doesn't suffer from sexlessness but from genital nostalgia. He dreams or daydreams, getting so close to psychedelia that anyone might think he smokes something strange. I understand him little.

Textographies of José

01

My soul is a kite made of palm sticks glued with cassava starch, that rises by tying its long string to a love, to a memory. If I can't find something to anchor it to, the winds of destiny will drag it in a wild sway, and I'll be just another one with a tangled soul in this war. (Subcomandante Buendía).

Life passes and we leave parts of it everywhere, maybe that's why we humans have this constant urge to go back to pick up something forgotten, to return to a place, to a person. And some, like me, risk-takers, utopians, anti-paradoxical, want to return to a time, not considering that we are no longer the same; time with its entropy has diluted skin and feelings, but even so, I want to go back and see you diagonally from my seat, with your perfectly ironed pleated uniform, your ponytail without a single strand of hair out of place, your black eyes, your brown skin, and your dove-like smile. How the hell do doves smile? I know doves don't, but you smile as they should. I think I remember how you smell; you smell of my entire past: fresh milk in the calambucos, sugar mangoes we picked between Retén and Aracataca, the sugar-coated tamarind balls from the cachaco's store, the first bite of guava, freshly cut grass in the clearings, you mix them all, purify them, and contrary to the unhealthy water of my town's aqueduct, you bathed and smelled of everything I miss today.

What you are now and what I am, I don't like. I don't want to talk anymore about your pot-bellied husband and my bisexual girlfriend; you already told me about his gas and his back hair, I already told you that last week (for the fourth time in two months) I found Julianita, my petite and short girlfriend, in a sexual act with two fat lesbians who looked at me with hatred, with the resentment of phallic envy, who looked like two hippos trying to get through a narrow door at the same time, and my girlfriend in the middle. I told you they didn't stop and that I didn't find it erotic at all, that Julianita extended her hand to me to join that destruction of aesthetics, but I, like someone fleeing a dogfight, preferred to go to the bathroom to look at myself in the mirror, to see if there was the time machine I have asked for again and again every Christmas.

She loves me, your kids love you, your flatulent husband loves you. Maybe life just needs cosmetic measures, like your husband shaving, taking Finigax, and my girlfriend improving her taste in women. Here I am talking to your memory, looking for a place to tie my kite, because I don't like what we are now.

02

I remember my mom telling me that with the first rains we couldn't bathe, and the rattle of the immense Caribbean drops on the zinc roofs, the flooded yards, and the girls in wet clothes shouted to me that one day I would miss them. The brown fish and the miracles that fall in every rain of my town decided to cease existing; they were the first casualties of a war that oblivion is winning... the trains of the Magdalena continue, carrying in their cars, the piled-up dead from past and future massacres...

03

It's been a while since I've heard horses galloping at night, nor does my mattress breathe like a ruminant beast, and besides, the house goblin returned the spoons without grumbling and without smudging them with soot. It seems that burning Carranza's old poems really was the cure for neuroses and witchcraft as Alicia said... But behind every cure, something dies and vice versa.

04

A planet, with a beach and a view of a horizon flatter

than the minds of the Catholic Monarchs, where horses and dogs sit to watch stupid humans run with bewilderment while eating marshmallow shells, and pretty girls don't want your kidneys to pay for their breast implants. There, my friend, we will sit and drink lemonade and think that all the ships come from China with their cheap t-shirts and their intellectual rats that die in cauldrons without telling their stories and their secrets to cure styes.

05

Something is split in two, somewhere someone is counting, another is planning how to steal one of the parts, I, I try to unite them, glue them together, and another one sees me and tells me the story of the milkmaid and the spilled milk. While I try to repair the damage, I think about how much I hate fleeting wise men, impertinent teachers, don't tell me anything, I know there's no solution, but... I won't be the first, and much less the second, to die trying. You still don't understand me and you're already realizing that I'm just trying to dizzy you with words, that you're the rubber duck rocking in this sea of loneliness. You can keep saying that what I write is pure shit, but at least credit me that it doesn't smell bad. Okay, I exaggerate, a sea of loneliness is too much for a nobody like me, let's leave it at a wave pool of melancholy in a recreational center. Happy now?

06

I don't know if it's appropriate to talk to you about my pains, yes, this time it's the pains, not loneliness, that's already a dry wound (it has scabs). Let me tell you these things while the world goes crazy outside, while gays and lesbians fight to get married and we absurdly fight to separate, while I feed the termites you passed to me in your saliva, in your flavors, mmm your flavors, that's precisely what I wanted to talk to you about... they hurt!

Patient 008

Don Tulio is a retiree from the University of

Antioquia. He likes very young women, was born in San Andrés, and traded the paradisiacal island for thermodynamics and the mountains of this turbulent valley. He wants to die now but can't bring himself to do it. He came to me through my friend, "the nymphomaniac of singledom." She slept with him when he was her professor. She is the best thing that has happened to him in his old age; after exhausting the mysteries and pouring out the programmed dose of testosterone per female, they became great friends. He now loves her like a daughter, and she loves him like a father who understands that her soul is lost and does not judge her.

Textographies of Tulio

01

Solitude, as beautiful as death, they resemble each other, gift coincidences to each other, and confuse their lovers. Many times, it is difficult to know if you are following the nostalgic ritual of death or if it is simply the anonymous steps of the solitary. Today I returned to my university. Ten years ago, I left it, maybe I'm here to retrace my steps to die, maybe I'm here to add more steps to this solitude. I believe it's the latter, because if I've honed anything in these years, it's my detector for virgins and depraved ones; death remains a virgin even though many braggarts of resurrections, reincarnations, and hallucinated lights at the end of tunnels say otherwise.

How I detest those who boast of corrupting, if they knew that we seasoned perverts are ruminants who chew memories over and over again, on a bus, on the train, in a class, in a gym, and we have our mental orgasms when the secret turns to vapor and makes us blush. But solitude, that one, everyone handles it, even me, who enters and exits from its depths to its skin and vice versa, sometimes even in involuntary spasms. My detector tells me that today I am with solitude, that this breath of lust is not from death.

It's Saturday, but the university is more alive than ever; there are children everywhere, swarming like microorganisms at the beginning of time. They come to play sports or engage in the arts, to prepare for life or rather for the shell we've made of it, because for life they are more than ready; there are young people in their classes fulfilling their dose of stagnation and, of course, the adults who accompany their children so that they may be several times happier than they were. My university looks beautiful to me: it is immense, I have the feeling of having entered a temple, that there are no sad people here although many yawn in the classrooms; I think I could live here, and, in fact, some do. I walk towards the football field which, fortunately and surely due to the rector's fear of riots, chains, and hunger strikes, is still not synthetic: the grass covering it calls for running and playing football, although I'm not very fond of it.

The dealers are under the beautiful ceiba tree that provides shade to the exercise bars, grinding with their hands the already ground marijuana leaves. As they do so, they salivate copiously and anxiously, showing that part of the business profits are consumed by them in product. A girl with a good body and a horrible face helps the dealer, she is in charge of rolling the joints. She has a book that I would swear is from the library and from it she tears pieces of paper where she skillfully sprinkles the leaves as if they were chicken broth, wraps them, rolls the ends, and moistens the edges to seal them. She has about three rolled; suddenly she is seized by a raucous, uncontrollable cough, thunderous and crashing; she spits out huge, bloody green phlegm, regains her composure, and continues rolling the funny cigarettes. She checks them and, saliva not being enough, blows on them to remove the tiny shavings that have stuck outside (The potential tuberculosis contagion is the adrenaline component of their joints). I exercise on the bars and all my joints crack. I am rusty like my thoughts. Pride makes me lift my body again and again to not be humiliated in front of the young people who do it naturally.

A little time passes, and the dealer's first customers arrive: three guys and a girl. She doesn't fit the surroundings; she's wearing a formal, black, tight-fitting outfit, vertiginous heels, well-done makeup, and a ceremonial hairstyle. They buy and sit on the bleachers of the field. They are closet potheads, bringing all their gadgets to hide their addiction: cigarette holders to avoid staining their fingertips, eye drops, mints, and a strong perfume.

I keep thinking about the girl in the evening dress and imagine having sex with her while she gets high, though for a moment I sabotage my mini fantasy thinking it must be terrifying if in the middle of the act she goes crazy, has a paranoia attack, some schizoid episode, and bites my penis off. I'd rather not keep imagining and continue forcing my joints until tendinitis. In front of the bars on a flagpole, a long metal tube, a woman practices pole dancing. Her strength and skill surprise me, although it would be obvious and almost obligatory to have bad thoughts about her, I reaffirm that certain professions have become extremely inclusive; today not all models are pretty, not all cheerleaders are sexy, and not all pole dance practitioners cause erections. She, with her loose shorts, was showing more than I wanted to see. I sat on the wall of another planter where a small, thick mango tree provided delightful shade.

But after a while, another dealer of the hedonistic type arrived: he also had canned beer in a cooler full of ice. He opened the trunk of his car with large speakers blasting songs by Snoop Dogg and Dr. Dre, while he and his shirtless friends consumed and sold, immersed in their parody of gangster life. One of them watched me, picked a ripe mango, washed it, and approached to greet me. He gave me the mango. He did it kindly, but one knows it's a sort of warning. He doesn't imagine that I'm in favor of the legalization of marijuana, that humanity should recognize another lost battle against pleasures. Although I am aware that the effects of marijuana, while enhancing the genius of many, also exponentially increase the stupidity of those who already were, to a degree that before getting high was manageable. I ate the mango. It was sweet. I felt again that pleasure of sinking my teeth into the fruit and was transported to my addiction, to nostalgia, to a Caribbean full of fruit trees, friends to share them with, simple loves to offer them to, where being a charming prince consisted of having a green guava and a little bag of salt tied to the waist for the barefoot princess at the same time. That parasite of memories caught me, and I preferred to leave, to leave those who make my university beautiful. All those people broken inside, who search for themselves in their chemical paradises without ever finding themselves; but in their infinite journeys, they feed on defeats, which one by one form those little hills of triumph that protect the wanderers. Among those lost people, I feel good. The centered, the arrogant, are scripted, their social media joys, their smiles to show and not to feel, their perfect lives, are as boring, predictable, and shitty as the books by Green, Collins, and Rowling that damage more minds than the worst of drugs. I take the metro and think that loneliness goes with me and sixteen hundred others, I know by their looks: they are lost but pretend to know where they are going. Like me.

02

Today my town is celebrating. I try to listen to "sentimental absence" without nostalgia, writing any stupidity on Facebook to distract melancholy in these virtual labyrinths where my decency often gets lost. It doesn't work! Melancholy has the scent of a bloodhound and comes back easily, it's not as stupid as decency... I guess I'll stick to it to find my way back, like in the cat joke.

03

Whenever I say I'm leaving, I really leave. At least that fundamental part of me goes and throws pebbles into the sea, while shyly avoiding the crabs. The rest of me remains here, living like a king with the small fraction of itself that a city demands.

Patient 009

Adriana is a secretary, wears a nose piercing, lots of makeup, and has a hippie chic style. She talks about imperialism, consumerism, and other leftist issues but always goes to expensive places. She complains on social media about her job, but during the week, she dresses formally and doesn't use bad words. She was dating a married man and bragged about having the best relationship because she knew there were no possible ties. The truth is she misses him, and he is now dating a friend she introduced him to at a birthday party, where she fulfilled his fantasy of having a threesome. In front of him and her, she pretends to be mature and free, but the beasts of heartbreak are eating her guts with their blunt teeth.

Textographies of Adriana

01

I call it distance when I'm not where I should be, and I call it loneliness when I don't know where I should be. A vicious and damnable circle (read damnable slowly), a cycle of small storms, missed connections, anxieties, and self-absence. There's no need to be surprised; one is absent from oneself simply when one doesn't want to be there or when something else is living our life. Most of the time, we are not; we believe we are, and so we are the belief of being what we think we are. Tangled, right? I'm always like this when I try to avoid telling you directly that I miss you and then, without a snap of the fingers, suddenly I know where I am: lost.

02

A bird sings on a distant hill, I imagine I hear it, it knows I imagine it... And together we form an angel, it criticizes my weight, I criticize its lice... We both hate that our dreams unite... But we both hate what we are separately.

Patient 010

Lina is 16 years old. She married a 40-year-old truck driver when she was 14, a good and generous man who came to her village, Argelia-Antioquia, and relieved Lina's family of the costs of her existence. In some environments, it's like that; poverty in many ways forces them to prefer the unhappiness of their children over death by starvation. She is very beautiful. When her husband is working, traveling all over the country, she seeks out lovers. She likes red lingerie and anal sex. She dreams of becoming a great doctor, and her hands are soft. She heals, I can attest, but she's a terrible student. In school, she's always suspended for talking too much, and although she sleeps with her teachers, she never asks them to improve her grades. Her state exams are dismal, and thus she won't be able to get into university. I didn't want to point this out to her to avoid making her sad. She says that when she becomes a doctor, she will take her family out of that miserable farm, bring them to live in a huge house in the city, and take them on a plane to see the sea. I also didn't want to tell her that general practitioners now earn a pittance, that we've screwed up the country for her generation. She tells me her dreams, and they hurt me.

Textography of Lina

01

Lina has a nice ass, small breasts, and enormous wings, seven meters from tip to tip. Not metaphorical wings to be a woman with wings and be screwed by a dirty poet like Oliverio, none of that, real wings with long feathers; white and gray. Since she was a child, she asked for them, first as a spoiled and egocentric child (as if she were Pablo Escobar's daughter asking for unicorns). She would behead her few dolls and beg everyone, parents, grandparents, child gods, virgin Marys, wise men, Santa Clauses, Buddhas, Mohammeds, wishing wells, shooting stars, fortune cookies, witches, seers, necromancers, gypsies... to please give her wings. Today she got them after a pilgrimage on her knees to Monserrate; fasting to the Fallen Lord of Girardota; with a cilice bought from an antique dealer (supposedly belonging to Father Marianito) to the Virgin of Sabaneta. It cost her all the money she had saved for the breast augmentation. This morning, when she looked in the mirror, drowsy, with that sleep laden with disappointment, routine, and boredom, at 16 she already had the weariness of a worker who wakes up early to sell his life; but this time, before smelling her own breath to disgust herself and enjoy it, she saw her large wings in the mirror. She hesitated for a moment, smiled because she thought she was in an extremely vivid dream, then burst into tears, like those people who are allotted only a moment of happiness in life. Her mother was knocking on the bathroom door, shouting, "Lina, open up! What's wrong?" She opened the door, and her mother couldn't believe what she saw. She thought it was stupid to stick wings on herself and that maybe Lina was crazy or on some drug. She tried to take them off, but couldn't. "What kind of implant is this? What did you do?" she asked, already desperate.

"Mommy, leave me."

Both cried, both believed that it was a dream and that soon they would wake up; Lina probably dreamed that she had large wings and her mom realized it, and Lina's mom dreamed that she surprised her daughter with large wings. They waited together for time to pass, had breakfast, joked about serving bird food, and cried again between laughs over the absurd dreams. Night came, and they thought they would sleep within their dreams as if suddenly an oneiric loop or something similar could form. Lina slept, as little as she could, face down, the wings made her very hot. She woke up, and nothing changed; this wasn't a dream, or maybe it was. Isn't life a long dream? They decided to take a taxi and go to an open field (The taxi driver made jokes about the costume and, at 55, maliciously commented that he liked bird girls), to test them, to see if they were real, if they fulfilled their function. She got into the taxi as best as she could, sat sideways, bent in the back so the wings could fit. In the field, she extended them and felt a certain power, flapped and flew, tears of happiness streaming down her face. She was free; now she wished it wasn't a dream, the air hit her face, the wind hummed in her ears at full speed, and in her wings, she felt strength. She remembered her favorite book, Jonathan Livingston Seagull, venturing to the highest point and diving down. Mom trembled with fear, shouting at her to be careful, but if it was a dream, there was no possibility of dying, she told herself.

She made very high flights and promised herself to return tomorrow and fly to the sea. That night, again, she couldn't sleep; the wings got in the way, she was used to sleeping on her back and the wings wouldn't allow it. Showering wet her feathers, and they took a long time to dry, producing a damp clothes smell that drove her crazy. This time, she was able to fly from home, and estimating where north was, she flew and flew. The patchwork quilt formed by the different colors of the crops brought her a well-being that made her forget the lack of sleep. Then the mountains, thick with trees that, when approached, revealed wonderful animals, the inhospitable jungle filled her with fascination. On the horizon, the land began to flatten, the mountains disappeared, and the plains moved her: how much solitude they produced, how much peace she felt observing them, the smell of the sea was felt or sensed, she didn't know if desire was playing a trick on her, but half an hour of flying over those hot lands, she saw the blue line of the ocean, cried as much as when she realized she had wings. She landed on a deserted beach, next to a little-traveled road; the sand was not fine, but somewhat rocky; the waves were strong and wetted her feet like a cat rubbing against her.

She stepped into the water, feeling algae underfoot, the sliminess producing a kind of pleasant disgust; her wings got soaked, she didn't care, but she couldn't swim underwater like she enjoyed in the pool and rivers. They weren't shaped for hydrodynamics, they were a drag in the depths. She had to open them to the sun, and even so, after two hours, the smaller feathers inside hadn't dried yet. Soon it would be dark, the sea began to chop, giving that primal, ancestral sensation of being in imminent danger, of the end of the world, perhaps memories of floods that never happened, floods that have tormented us from the caverns of our souls. She managed to take off, though they were a bit heavy, but with flapping, they dried. She got home, where her mom was waiting, worried. The boy she liked was there, a jester who always wore shorts and a cap, but she adored him. They went up to her room to listen to music and have sex, but they couldn't; he couldn't get an erection, something didn't fit in the anatomy of desire for that skinny jester. She told him it was normal, that it happened to everyone. He slapped his member and tried to think of Esperanza Gómez, the Colombian porn star, but even that didn't manage to inflate his apparatus. He went home defeated, crying; she stayed there crying. He never had an erection with a girl again, the fear of not having one became an obsession and he couldn't concentrate. She tried to forget and sleep, but couldn't; she was already desperate with everything, with not being able to bathe properly, not being able to shit properly, not being able to have sex, tripping over everything. She ended up hating her wings. She hated hating, hated now that her dreams were coming true and that she wasn't able to appreciate what she had. One day, she woke up without wings, without dreams. She was afraid to dream, not like some because of the danger that they wouldn't come true, but for the opposite reason.

Patient 11

Diego lives next to the sports center in Bello and does yoga in jeans because his fat doesn't look good in the sportswear the other practitioners use. He's been studying at university for eight years, unable to finish his degree, repeating subjects, canceling, postponing, suffering from severe procrastination and, obviously, overwhelming loneliness. He claims to be proud of it, but it's clear he longs for love, though he warns that he's not relationship material. He's had the experience a thousand times, and what begins with fairies farting rose-scented gas is simply a trap for species preservation, a complex mating ritual for a complex animal. And then, once the ritual is consummated, the lethargy and apathy are uncontrollable, and thus come the weeping and gnashing of teeth. He pretends to be happy with his loneliness. He has discovered ingenious masturbation techniques, manages a social media profile called "Masturbation Techniques for Happiness," but he's not happy. There he gives tips on how to make holes in watermelons to stick the penis into, how to heat papayas so that when you insert the penis it perfectly simulates body warmth; and he has shared his post about masturbating with a banana peel about 32 times. But he's not happy. And like many, even without recognizing it, he doesn't know where happiness is either. He just wants to know where it is, that would be enough, he doesn't need to feel it.

Textographies of Diego

01

The lonely ones are the horse with the long tongue that reaches the carrot and then stops walking, the caterpillar that never leaves the chrysalis, and the angel with leaden wings. We are the unit that survived the fractions, the stick that breaks piñatas, the salmon that tells its fish friends how it got its claw scars. But all that display of strength slides down the Saturday night slide, when TV shows become sad, the five-thousand-peso Hawaiian pizza slice has too much pineapple, and you bombard yourself with the apparent happiness of social media. Everything crumbles then, and afterward, like a disciplined Japanese after a disaster, with dignity and in silence, you pick up your mess; the clothes scattered on the floor, the crumbs of food, you throw away receipts in silence, and try to edit the photos you took in bed putting on a face that to you is sexy and to others is the graphic description of constipation. On Monday, work distracts you. The world with its speed makes you dizzy and doesn't let you die, you fear the weekend, during the workday you are not alone, you flirt with everyone and think it's possible something might happen, but everyone has an excuse and you have yours too. Days turn into weeks, weeks into months, and months into years. Your guts are no longer the same, dandruff has become resistant, and your desires increasingly realistic.

02

I'm afraid to dream about you. Not because of the dream, but because of what I'll feel afterward, upon waking, when I realize I have drool, eye crust, an erection, bad breath, and not you. When I realize the world is as real as the pillow seam marks on my face. When I realize that dreaming about you is a humiliating consolation prize because the grand prize perhaps went to some jackass, who will see your face upon waking – which, with all certainty – with drool, eye crust, and bad breath will look otherworldly, celestial. I exaggerate intentionally to not fall short with the right words. I've never dreamed about the one I like. When asked, I rhetorically say I have, but I lie. Even with those precedents, I beg not to dream of you; with the years, my tolerance for frustration has decreased, I can bear defeat, but not frustration, you know. Frustration is based on an illusion, a self-deception, while defeat, my dear, is for the strong. I'll tell you a secret that makes me seem crazy: sometimes I think the people in dreams also sleep, and when they do, they dream. Right at that moment, we wake up, and they dream of us. So, who are real, them or us? Well, now I've officially added madness to sentimentality and distanced myself further, riding wild, untamed words running in the opposite direction of everything I want. To professionalize my self-pity, I'll say that destiny charges me more for everything. I bid you goodnight, it's late, I hope you have an erotic and twisted dream about me, disturbing, so that in some way you also have your punishment, although not wanting isn't punishable.

03

Silence returns, with its phlegm-like texture, with its morning breath; accepting a "no" is an art I've mastered, applying the old trick of displacing the pain to places other than the heart. It hurts the same, but not in the same spot. Dad used to say: "Move it to your head, shoulders, stomach... But don't be such a pussy to move it to your dick... Because then you'll never forget." Dad is rough, coarse, raw, but he knows what he's talking about. I learn easily, with the ease of those who fear dick pain.

04

I know what kind of monster love turns into – Diego would say – it's a dragon pup, cute, tied to your finger with vine chains. One day at six in the morning, its breath turns foul, and its hair gets messy. Now it drags you with anchor chains, listens to you cry alone, and though it knows the reasons, it doesn't look at you while filling out its umpteenth vanity test, man's ashes, evaporated tears, and dried blood. Unintentionally, love turns into a monster, and you become a witch's pantry. Love eats sad men and spits out dissatisfied women. That's what monsters do... Men, men go back to chaining little dragons with vines.

Patient 012

Diana, everyone likes Diana; she's funny and sweet, the soundtrack of her life is "In Some Place" by Duncan Dhu, especially the part that says... "and in the shadows, geniuses die without knowing their magic"... She wrote a book for her daughter, she's a single mother, criticized her mom for not being able to give her a normal home, for separating from her father who sixty percent of the time was a good man. She left her husband because she caught him touching her drunken friend's breasts when she slept over after a party. The book she wrote for her daughter is a fantasy of beautiful things, ideal worlds, and characters that piss rainbows. She looks for faithful but not boring men, serious but not prudish, passionate but with conservative prejudices, cheerful but not talkative, handsome but not vain, sporty but not fanatic. Evidently, she's alone, no one has told her, but she's looking for herself. Her only flaw is not accepting the flaws of others.

Textographies of Diana

01

Watching my daughter as she plays, so sure, while she flits about, I find it impossible to remember the point at which, being so perfect, we turned into this, into adults. They call it growing up, but it surely only refers to height. Humanity clings to the pinnacle of evolution, while the simple caterpillar, over time, slaps our arrogance by transforming into an imposing butterfly, and we, so haughty, so magnificent, turn into ourselves, born infinite and becoming a singular unit, just one.

02

Spring fairies, smashed against windshields, splash on the wipers; the grumpy ones pay 500 pesos at traffic lights to displaced dark-skinned kids to clean the rainbow mess these damn fairies leave on their luxury cars. It's not enough for them to sprout little flowers on the sidewalks of Poblado to be trampled by the expensive shoe of a politician's son. Now, with their little sunshits, they want to ruin the perfect winter, the perfect gray...

03

How do I tell that little girl I once was not to dream anymore? That the night was made for sleeping… that the witches on the rooftops sit to swallow the essence of the future with pinches of pepper and salt, and spit out chimeras into the eyes of cats that mate with pain... Don't dream anymore... Go and pluck the lilies from the garden, sleep on them... Breathe them in and wish me good luck.

Patient 013

John is a resentful man. He has a nice house by the Boston park, wears branded sneakers, and has a job where he earns good commissions by trapping the gullible in the multi-level marketing scheme. But he's over 30 now, couldn't study, and had big dreams: to be an astronaut, to change the world, to perform duets with Cerati at Madison Square Garden, and to reject the Oscar for Best Actor as an act of rebellion against the commercialization of the seventh art. Here he is, trapped in a common life that has become a prison, surviving by boasting about dubious conquests and frivolous spending. But he confides in me, tells me he feels like a nobody, that his secret of having kissed a transvestite one drunken night lowers his self-esteem.

Textographies of John

01

(No country for old men) One random day, you look out the window of the bus. It's raining, and small drops are crashing against the glass. Outside, people are running for cover, the highway is slow, and that's dangerous—you have more time to think, and that's fatal. You spot the huge billboard for a men's perfume, the model is a brawny young guy, the kind you'll never be because your genes surely have some donkey DNA tangled in them, and you've reached that age where, according to your plans, all dreams and fantasies should have already been fulfilled. You're on a bus, sitting next to an obese person who's pushing you against the window with his bulk, and you realize that unless an interstellar war with rapist aliens breaks out, there's no way you'll ever be an astronaut. Besides, the only vehicle you barely know how to drive is a bicycle. It's out of the question to even think about taking pictures in a space shuttle. The fat guy next to you tries to pull some coins out of his tight pocket to buy candies from one of the many vendors aged by the sun and pollution. The fat guy wedges his elbow into my ribs in his piggish effort to extract the money, his breathing makes noises, and he hums an AC/DC song. It's even noisier when he eats, and I feel more miserable. I recognize the AC/DC song and let out a sigh because, for the same reasons I won't be an astronaut, I won't be a rock star either: I only recently found out that major and minor notes exist, my voice sings everything in a single tone, without inflections, and guttural sounds give me a sore throat. There's a minor accident on the highway, we pass slowly, there's another billboard, now a beautiful woman in the photo. Fucking life! – I think, I'll never sleep with a woman like that. At this age, I attract worn-out divorcees who break the ice with comments about the weather and the little clothing needed in the heat. Divorcees whose apathy and bad experiences have lowered their standards from the popular rich, intelligent prince charmings to simply accepting someone who can at least brush his teeth twice a day. It doesn't flatter you that they talk to you; it makes you feel more rotten because you know you're the resignation of a disappointed and lonely woman.

At the northern terminal, a stunning, almost impossible girl boards the bus. I gaze at her from her thighs up to her eyes as she looks for a seat, and there's a whale next to me. We exchange glances; my eyes fix on her and penetrate, but she quickly avoids my gaze, not because she feels invaded, but because I'm just some guy on a bus. From a distance, you can tell she's the kind who rides on the back of her boyfriend's high-powered motorcycle and posts photos on social media sipping extravagant cocktails in Lleras, Cartagena, San Andrés, Cancún. She's one of those pretty girls from the lower class (you can tell) with upper-class boyfriends who take them out of these lost neighborhoods and return them as the worn-out divorcees I don't like (Chronos and his untimely fuckeries). But now she's uncomfortable with a guy who's undressing her with his eyes, mainly because he's just a guy on a bus. It's also too late to make money; I took the rocky path to glory, and there's no turning back on that road, nor any guarantee of reaching the goal. The path to money is simpler—if you walk it, you'll surely get it—but the path to glory is all or nothing. In my case, nothing. And I'm getting to that age where you start buying lottery tickets and trying to find magic formulas to win, where you know that glory belched in your face after eating chorizo, and you resign yourself to the hope that chance provides. The pretty girl gets off near the Coca-Cola factory, looking up to avoid meeting anyone's gaze; I also look the other way. I have my dignity as a poor and ugly man, even though the muscles around my eyes and neck cramp up with the contradictory orders from my brain.

This seems like a day forewarned by Cioran, although I know that Cioran himself would console me by saying that, in any case, death is near, and that there is no difference between the frivolous success touted by this society and the happiness of flies finding a pile of dung.

02

A gnome, one of those that look under skirts and seem like dogs in heat, was crying inconsolably, leaning against the heels of a beautiful blonde in a blue dress. Since I like talking to strange people, I asked him what was wrong, but with the fear that he might rob me or ask for alms (here they don't kill us with enchantments)

– it's this fucking modernity – he said... Now they all wear shorts and if they don't, it's because they're transvestites. I tried not to laugh because it was evident that the blonde shaved her beard, so I offered him gum, shook his little gnome hat, and said: these are tough times for fantasy... And I walked away thinking that we were both in the wrong era.

Patient 014

Mauricio lives in Sabaneta. It's difficult to say anything about him. His main flaw is that there's nothing to say about him. He is the standard type, with standard height, standard weight, an average salary, normal intelligence—neither outstanding nor poor. He dresses in clothes from chain stores, the same as everyone else. Well, there is one thing that characterizes him: everyone else who comes to tell me their stories, even I, would like to be like him. He has no pretensions, his life is scripted, and he will die without thinking about it. The doses of pain and happiness are measured, balanced. He is a damn normal being, whom those of us living in crisis will always envy. But he is friends with Diana, so I listened to his vain attempts to be interesting, but I am entirely sure that what he told me is not his story, not his thoughts. It is the emphatic side of the trivial. I will tell what he said with the intention that someone real recognizes their lost world in these words. Now that I think about it, there is a differentiating factor in him: he is a fraud. Such a common being cannot be "What loneliness wants to be when it grows up."

Textographies of Mauricio

01

I woke up with the purifying sensation of having cried while sleeping, and it must have been so because of the feeling of calm and the absence of an erection. I dreamed of an unknown woman, but in the dream, I loved her desperately, and she didn't love me. She dreamed of another stranger whom she loved madly, and he didn't love her either. He, in turn, dreamed of another stranger... And so on infinitely. I had the certainty that love is a hamster on its exercise wheel, running and running, panting, biting, and getting nowhere. The distance is so immense for our fat rat brains... Just when the dream turned and I would know which stranger loved me, I woke up with a start, <<the

wheel sometimes comes loose>>... I'll better continue with my life as a street rat.

02

I am the echo of a man who screams before your abysses, the wave that crashes against hard walls of supernatural rock, the echo that repeats for years, on the bus, in front of the TV, buys rice, vegetables, and pays the bills. The echo writes, tears up, misses, and his beard doesn't grow evenly. The echo is dying, and the concrete man moves away from the precipice, whistles a familiar tune with his hands in his pockets, walking to find another wall to crash his existence against, like an exercise in futility, a way to mark a nebulous and cold territory, the felled forest of broken loves.

03

(What loneliness wants to be when it grows up) The "what does that guy have?" I want to be that in your life, the rumor that arises when they see us, what does that guy have, read on the lips that speak in hushed tones, be the curiosity that corrodes them, the mating mathematics that don't add up, what is a 10 doing with a 5 rounded with artifices, with invented residues? I want to be the surprise when they find out that I am just an average—average intelligence, average salary, average penis, average tongue, average dreams. They will never know that my secret with you is that I have lost everything, and therefore, fearing to lose you doesn't make me anxious; that my relationship with limbo makes you sick with mystery, that in my existential drift and my dizziness, I could love you today with superlative totality and tomorrow upon waking, you might bother me like a misshapen pillow. That vertigo fascinates you because some hidden masochism cloaks all self-sufficiency. That what you like about me is that I have no certainty about anything at all, that I am what loneliness wants to be when it grows up, the leftover particle, the burr of the universe, the crumbs of paradise gathered by demons to form their little hells, the significance of pubic hair in the invention of the light bulb. I want to be "what does that guy have?", at least for a while until I get tired of your perfection, of your fair proportions, of your symmetry and measure, of the clear and fluid things, of your springtime love and the horrifying possibility of a huge and lasting happiness.

04

You like him, I understand, his words are easy, and the mind is a cyclist going downhill: it avoids effort and pain. You don't like me, I understand that too, my sentences are full of abysses and twists where you can still hear echoes of distress. He writes anything, and you value the effort of the lines filled with cheap, crude, unfortunate poetry, like pigeon shit on your white blouse, falling on you in Parque Berrío. Well, my love isn't simple, there is drama, a certain slavery, darkness, misalignments, perversion, and the envy you're noticing. When you want to complicate things, find me, for even though I'm lost, I'll be where you point, in the same place we don't know, at the same time we'll never meet, a step away from the greeting we won't give each other.

Patient 015

Marcos lives in a common-law marriage with Damaris and doesn't know how to tell her that he no longer loves her, that monotony and daily life consume him, that he has suffered a lot in his life, that the country's war has touched him with its burning trident, he collects heartbreaks like disgusting people collect boogers on the walls... Damaris was born to have a perfect life: work, buy a car, a house, have children, go to family parties, and bake cookies. He is full of devastating insomnia, while she sleeps peacefully beside him; she simplifies Marcos' worries by giving him spa coupons, and she will never understand that an electrical technician for eight years in the same company wants something more from life than life itself (Marcos thinks the solution is another woman; he met Cindy, but Cindy doesn't want him, which is why he stays with Damaris, although he won't admit it).

Textographies of Marcos

01

I highly value my rubble, every pain, every tear, every despair, each of those broken pieces that pile up on the walls of the "self." It's as if I'm applying the strategy of diamond merchants, breaking a huge one into pieces to gain more profit. That's why I don't give myself to you, you are complete inside and out. It's not that you are worth less because of the diamond thing, it's that you wouldn't understand how many disasters and wars I have survived. We would be so lonely together, you wouldn't bear my lost looks when you talk to me, my insomnia, my hatred, my displaced resentments, you wouldn't even understand what I'm writing here. There are destinies, they say. I don't believe in them, they are nonsense for mental slackers, but there is a certain mockery in events and, to continue with self-sabotage, I'll tell you that I need someone who, like me, lives by masking their wreckage, imploding every day, inverting meanings every day. You see: loneliness is that ability to become too specific.

02

I get excited by women who share my disinterests, my tedium, my disgusts, my unimportant world; those who have the same tastes as me are boring, and by transitivity, so am I; common and predictable like reciprocated love.

03

My love is normal, like a man's, like a human's, like having coffee while looking into the distance in a narrow café... Full of unfathomable realities, like how today I won't dream of you no matter how hard I try, and possibly in the rush of dawn, I won't remember how you look in the mornings. I look at other women and imagine unspeakable, unpublishable, and unforgivable things in eight religions, and after so many repeated scenes, guilt died in some poorly executed, sacrilegious, or profane attempt.

But just before sleeping, when I say goodnight to you, I wish I wasn't myself, to become ideal, the promise made to you, the one who arrives in the end on a horse, with fireworks and prancing little animals. But I swear that even though I've worked hard to be who I am, it hasn't been intentional.

04

...and in those senseless acts that characterize me, I

unjustly wish you would treat me better than I treat the person I don't like. I agonize in late responses, in syllabic stinginess, in conciseness, in concreteness, in hurtful politeness, in the lack of gaps where my possibilities might squeeze in. And I wish I detested you less than the person I don't like detests me, but I'm probably also boasting about being a better hater. How selfish we are when we love and how damn cruel when we don't. Recognizing it doesn't relieve me. Recognizing it doesn't relieve her. Recognizing it doesn't make us any less miserable, writing it doesn't absolve me, reading it doesn't unsettle you, and the landscape of forgetfulness proudly opens beyond the hills of the angels' excrement, from where unrequited loves silently leap in an automatic, digitized suicide.

Patient 016

The Lovely Francisca, 33 years old, personal trainer, talks about coaching and other bullshit of existential crises that greedy money thinkers have managed to commercialize. She has the respective surgeries, the general loneliness. She lives in Laureles, in an apartment inherited from her mother; her husband owns a small store selling dietary supplements for athletes. He no longer tells her she's beautiful, she no longer tells him he's big.

Textographies of the Lovely Francisca

01

<<This can't be>> said Francisca, lying face down, naked, staring at the headboard of the bed, while trying to scratch her name into the wood with her nails. It was the ninth time they had sex, it was the ninth time she repeated that this couldn't be... She feels guilty. Her husband is a good husband, even though they no longer go out for a drink, dance in the dark, and he no longer says sweet things to her. He prepares her meals, nutritious shakes, and picks her up from work even though she gets out at 10 p.m. and he at 6 p.m. The man beside her lies on his back, caressing his flaccid penis, smiling; she's eating out of his hand (not precisely out of his hand). He looks like Cerati and sings in a band that performs cheap and out-of-tune covers of Soda Stereo. That excites her. Her husband has caught her touching herself while looking at the poster of the great Gustavo.

02

Having lost the war against pleasures, all that's left is to ask for forgiveness from our dead and pray that hell is nothing more than the name of a Mexican nightclub. We gave in, we disarmed, we undressed, and then we were lethal. I learned to fly low, we learned, and as we forget everything, I remember you again. I don't walk, we don't walk, we fly close to the ground, and as dad would conclude: "my girl... we live close to the ground!"

03

Oh yes, my generation knew pubic hair and heterosexual pop singers and dreamed that in the year 2000 Jesus would descend, or extraterrestrials would arrive with the cure for venereal diseases. Today we hope that any prophecy will come true (it doesn't matter which, but let something come true), meanwhile... A sigh, white noise, and lots of light music. (may some animal force raise Cerati).

Patient 17

José, 46 years old, looks young. He is the typical hyena, laughs, mocks, but is a crying clown. He looks strong, but melodramatically corners himself in the bathroom to cry while water runs over his hairy body; he lives with his parents and siblings. He gets drunk, and his megalomania sprouts; then he says he knows the mayor and the president, has killed hundreds who dared to contradict him, and has more money than Bill Gates. Deep down, he knows he is a loser and tells me so, but he wipes his tears, and immediately the infuriating know-it-all appears. He seems to suffer from a split personality, an unfortunate bipolarity not conceived by the writer Robert L. Stevenson. A poor hairy man with two terrible personalities. Two Mr. Hydes in one body.

Textographies of José "The Hyena"

01

Butt Therapy (Real Story Based on Real Butts). Today, December 26th, I was at the gym doing some cardio when a man came to my side, moving from machine to machine, telling everyone that his girlfriend had dumped him on December 24th. He was heartbroken and furious, "How dare she leave me on Christmas?" I heard everyone giving him the usual advice in these situations, feeding his dead hopes: don't worry, she'll come back, you're a great person, and a whole series of consoling rhetoric, detectable from miles away. I overheard all of this by chance; normally, I'm very focused on some butt as therapy to not feel the rigor of the exercise, but on December 26th, it was just a few of us men trying to regain the self-esteem that the mirror crushes. And this poor guy came to do cardio next to me; I laughed to myself, like carnivorous plants must laugh when an insect lands right in their mouth to ruin their life. He greeted me, and I waited, with pre-weariness, for him to find a way to vent, and so he did. <<You gotta work out to snag a hot chick because when you're single...>>, he said, and continued with the story of his breakup. He showed me pictures of the girl and wanted me to console him, but anyone who knows me even a little knows that my soul is raw, it throbs like a sore, splashes like a salmon in a bear's mouth. So, in the five minutes I had left on the elliptical, I said: <<look, cousin, from the photos you showed me, she's not very pretty. She always takes photos from the same angle and in the same pose, meaning the rest of the angles must be bad. Several of the photos are in different cars of a higher range than yours, indicating she's the authentic Eve. You've read the Catholic Bible, I suppose? It says that Eve, despite being in Paradise, remained dissatisfied, and that's why she fell and made Adam fall into temptation. The Bible, cousin, is the first anthropological study that exists, and what it really shows is that women will always be dissatisfied, and I'm not judging, but it's their genetic mandate: always seeking a generous and prosperous provider for their offspring. Obviously, she'll always try to be with the one who assures her descendants a possible and comfortable survival, which is why she fights like a lioness against others of her kind to secure her male, her territory; that's her function. On the other hand, the man's role is that of a provider and reproducer, which is why we're always thinking about taking half of humanity to bed (just half, for those of us with good taste; the whole for those who will nail anything). For that simple reason, they seek prosperity and we seek butts. Now, there's always one who will say she doesn't want someone with money, but to grow financially alongside a fighter and other mental nonsense. Those are the worst, cousin, because they will embark you on a mad race to achieve things that you don't give a damn about, and they will nag you daily for the rest of your filthy and absurd life in an incessant hassle. But, I repeat, it's pure genetics; if they don't do

it, you won't move to provide what they need, because if it were up to you, you'd live only to reproduce. That's why I think she won't come back. Take a photo next to Juan's truck and she'll probably call you, otherwise, I see the reunion as unlikely. And I added: the right thing in a country like this, where the economy fluctuates, political conditions fluctuate, and crime doesn't fluctuate, is that women should choose intelligent men for their ability to adapt to changes, because even if they fall into terrible ruin, they will rise again. Even if a war or a catastrophe strikes – but we are still years away from that – ultimately, each gender protects what their ancestral, primary, original mandate orders them to; and although they don't coincide, they allow humanity to exist and grow. As for love – I continued more fluently than ever, almost salivating and licking each word – it is a psychological construct, although many things make it seem otherwise. We are the most evolved species, and we not only manufacture physical and concrete things but also create psychic frameworks that allow us to organize and continue. The heartbroken guy got off the elliptical, bewildered, and lay down on the aerobics stage to look at his phone. I know he'll call her; losing the herd is painful and terrible for some. In animals, many die when they lose it, but if a stronger male beats you, what can we do? Just as I was leaving, relieved of the poison of reality I had poured into that poor guy, a girl with an incredible leotard walked in. I glanced at her furtively as always, and left. Today was a gym day without butt therapy.

02

...and we were never more important than now that we have nothing, and no one expects much from us... It is in loss that freedom writhes, in its gelatinous condition and its relative truths... Sitting here, talking about what could have been and the important people we know, who equal in number to those who don't remember us... We lack nothing, because even memories conspire against congenital guilt and recurring fears... Today we lack nothing because we have discovered that after so much pretending, nothing is possessable.

I don't know where this will lead, where the waves will take this shipwreck called life. We cling to anything that seems like a lifeline, even to childish exercises like telling stories, hoping that by some miracle in which we don't believe but still hope for, someone will give us the formula to nullify the constant anxiety; the perpetual perception and reflection on existence. We know beforehand that happiness lies in surrendering like a corpse bloated by gases to the current of this icy river called destiny; getting up early on Mondays, eating cereal, watching the news, saying for the umpteenth time that the news anchor Alejandra Santos is very hot, making double entendre jokes at the office, going back home, reinforcing the contamination of idiotic things caused by newscasts, making lunch for Tuesday, storing it in the lunchbox, praying the rice doesn't spoil, and sleeping without prior reflections. Repeating the same process daily until dying, also without noticing death. That is happiness, the selfishness of not living for anyone else, killing guilt with a clean stab and not deviating from the script we were given to perform.

Those who read Coelho and other merchants of hope will say there are flaws in my perspective because they are happy, and their idiocy comes from providers with higher rates. But ultimately: all these broken people who come to tell their imperfect life stories live in the real world.

Beginning

About the Author:

Efraín José Martínez Meneses was born in Fundación, Magdalena. Violence tore him away from the Macondian Caribbean and led him to the urban realism of Medellín. A professor and researcher, he received the Ibero-American Merit Award in Education and Research in 2015. He is the author of three books on education and the social reintegration of ex-combatants of the armed conflict, published in 2014, 2015, and 2016.

Despite never having visited Paris, he dares to write about love, sex, war, and misery in a dizzying and intense mix. In 2012, he published his first autobiographical book, "Butterfly Effect," a single-page work. Additionally, he has published three short stories in regional newspapers under absurd pseudonyms.

Martínez Meneses has two unpublished novels, "Subcomandante" and "The Dog that Didn't Sniff Butts," which will be published in 2024 and 2025. With shades of magical realism, he has been called "the last writer of Macondo," though his work also reflects the raw and existential influence of Bukowski and the tenderness of Sabines. Over time, he has become a cult writer, attracting a dedicated and passionate audience for his unique narrative style.

We are seeds of creation. And so it is that every dream, thought, or product of imagination, without intending to, becomes a new world. Created in places and times unknown to us. Obviously, we are the result of someone who dreamed us... and here we go adrift, creating with each blink universes as fluid as tears. (Subcomandante Buendía)

Call to Action

Continuing to support authors like Efraín José, who come from war and fury, and competing with the big publishers that sell satisfaction rather than truth and art, depends on your support. Thank you for purchasing the book, and thank you for reaching this point. It would be of immense value to us if, having enjoyed the book and found something significant in it, you left a review. Your opinion is crucial for more readers to discover this work and for us to keep sharing authentic and moving stories.

Thank you for your support!

www.ingramcontent.com/pod-product-compliance
Lightning Source LLC
LaVergne TN
LVHW091103150826
845673LV00002B/703

* 9 7 8 9 5 8 5 9 3 9 2 4 0 *